ABC DAY

Written by Dipti Joshi

Illustrated by Sarah Naberhaus

ISBN number 978-1-7328077-0-9 (Paperback Edition)
ISBN number 978-1-7328077-1-6 (Hardcover Edition)

Library of Congress Number 20188958868

Editing by ALBe and Nita Baum
Illustrations by Sarah Naberhaus

Printed in the United States of America
First printing February 2019

Published by SF&H, LLC

www.ABCDayBook.com

This is a throwback to the non-digital age when kids would get on their bikes without a helmet, eat lots of candy, and explore places on their own. In no way do we condone not wearing a helmet. It is the law in many states. Studies confirm the importance of wearing a helmet to significantly reduce chances of head injuries and brain trauma. This might be a good talking point and an opportunity to allow your kids to draw their own helmets on Derevia and her friends.

 One bright and sunny morning, Derevia, Judson, Gilles, and Silvento began their adventure.

Judson hit a rock and had an accident.

A is for Accident

Derevia pulled her first aid kit out of her backpack. They all helped to patch him up, and he was no longer crying.

A is for Aid

B is for Bluebirds

B is for Beach

B is for Bikes

While they rode their bikes to the beach, they saw bluebirds.

They stopped at their favorite candy store, Shore's Candy.

They bought dragon gummies, eel gummies, and five gumballs for later

C is for Candy

D is for Dragon

E is for Eels

F is for Five

G is for Gumballs

At the beach, they saw hermit crabs in the sand and honeybees in the air.

H is for Honeybees

H is for Hermit crabs

Shore's Candy

I is for Irises

They followed the bees to some irises.

Many different insects were flying around.

Derevia took out her jam jar and collected them.

I is for Insects

is for Jam Jar

Silvento reminded Derevia that she shouldn't keep them.

Derevia opened her jar and let the insects free.

Silvento flew his kite in the breeze.
Everyone else followed.

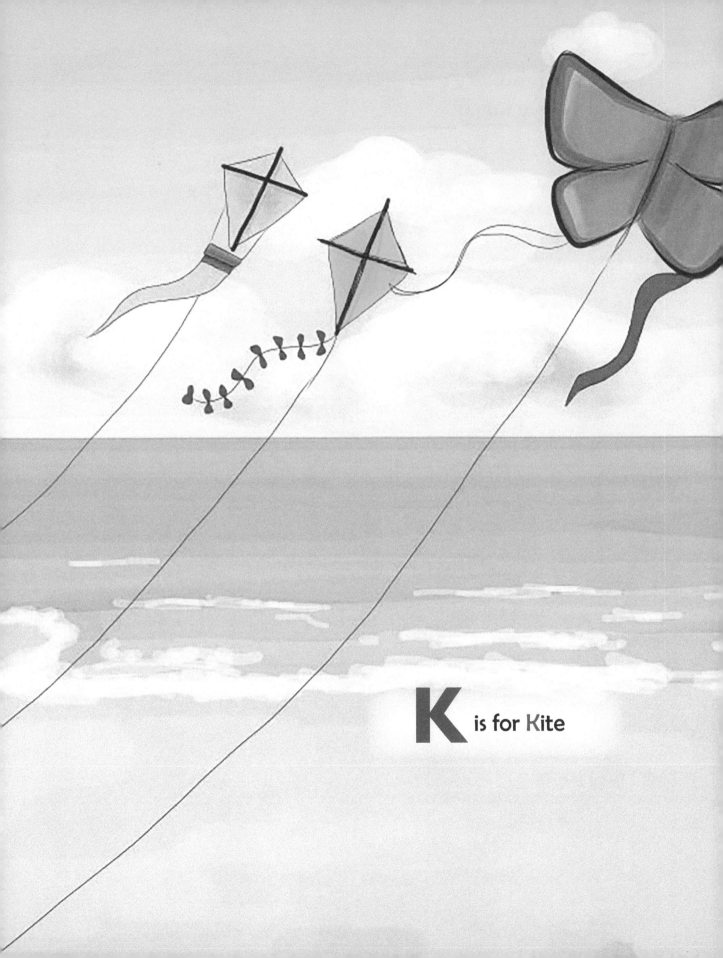

K is for Kite

Gilles was hungry and yelled,
"Let's have lunch!"

L is for Lunch

They ate their meal on a
magenta table.

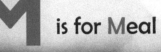

M is for Meal

M is for Magenta

Their friend, Nancy, walked to their table.

Derevia shared her delicious noodles with Nancy.

N is for Noodles

N is for Nancy

Olivia, another friend, brought peach popsicles for everyone.

O is for Olivia

P is for Popsicle

P is for Peach

After their meal, they all quickly
raced to the ocean.

Q is for Quickly

R is for Raced

They skipped over seashells
and starfish.

S is for Skipped

S is for Seashells

S is for Starfish

They swam in the turquoise ocean and saw many beautiful creatures underwater.

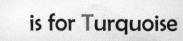

T is for Turquoise

U is for Underwater

After they swam, they said
goodbye to Nancy and Olivia.

Derevia, Judson, Gilles, and Silvento walked back to their bikes, which were parked beside beautiful violets and wavy grass.

V is for Violets

W is for Wavy

While walking their bikes along the path toward home, they heard a band playing the guitar, drums, and xylophone.

X is for Xylophone

CPSIA information can be obtained
at www.ICGtesting.com
Printed in the USA
BVHW021937291119
565205BV00003B/12/P

9 781732 807716